The Christmas Cookie Thief

By Meredith Rusu

SCHOLASTIC INC.

© 2018 Ty Inc. Used with permission of Ty Inc. TY and the TY Heart Logo are registered trademarks of Ty Inc. The trademark BEANIE BOOS™ is also owned by Ty Inc.

All rights reserved. Published by Scholastic Inc., *Publishers since 1920.* SCHOLASTIC and associated logos are trademarks and/or registered trademarks of Scholastic Inc.

The publisher does not have any control over and does not assume any responsibility for author or third-party websites or their content.

No part of this publication may be reproduced, stored in a retrieval system, or transmitted in any form or by any means, electronic, mechanical, photocopying, recording, or otherwise, without written permission of the publisher. For information regarding permission, write to Scholastic Inc., Attention: Permissions Department, 557 Broadway, New York, NY 10012.

This book is a work of fiction. Names, characters, places, and incidents are either the product of the author's imagination or are used fictitiously, and any resemblance to actual persons, living or dead, business establishments, events, or locales is entirely coincidental.

ISBN 978-1-338-25620-8

10 9 8 7 6 5 4 3 2 1   18 19 20 21 22

Printed in the U.S.A. 40
First printing 2018
Book Design by Becky James

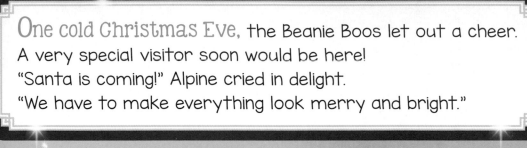

One cold Christmas Eve, the Beanie Boos let out a cheer.
A very special visitor soon would be here!
"Santa is coming!" Alpine cried in delight.
"We have to make everything look merry and bright."

2

Icicles the owl had to agree.
"The first thing to do is decorate the tree."
Quick as a flash, the Boos did as he said.
Soon the tree sparkled with gold, silver, and red.

"I want to help!" cried the little mouse, Mac.
"But first, how about a Christmastime snack?"
"Oh, Mac," Alpine giggled. "You think with your tummy!"
That little mouse was *always* quite hungry.

"But there's no time for nibbling," said Presents the pup.
"We have boxes to wrap and bows to tie up."
With paper and ribbon and glitter and string,
The Boos wrapped the gifts without missing a thing.

Mac wiggled his whiskers. "*Now* can we eat?
"My stomach is rumbling. It's time for a treat!"
"Treats!" Freeze the penguin cried with a gasp.
"Santa will be hungry when he gets here at last."

"Then we'll make him some nibbles." Alpine nodded his head.
"Cookies and candy and sweet gingerbread."
"Oooh," Mac whispered, licking his lips.
"Perhaps I could help with some pro baking tips?"

"Oh, Mac," said his friends. "You'll just wind up munching.
Keep a lookout for Santa, let us know if he's coming.
We promise we'll eat when the baking is through.
But right now there's no time—there's still so much to do!"

So off with a scurry Mac ran to the chimney.
Meanwhile the others got baking and busy.
"More peppermint!" said Candy Cane.
"More ginger!" said Freeze.
"And of course, eggnog ice cream. As much as you please!"

Mix went the mixer. *Ding* went the stove.
The treats kept on coming—a Christmastime trove!
Chocolate and marshmallows, sugar and spice.
Had treats for old Santa ever looked quite so nice?

"But wait!" came a cry from the reindeer named Comet.
"Look at my plate—there's nothing upon it!"
Comet was right. Though the baking was done,
Comet's gingerbread plate held nothing but crumbs.

Icicles frowned. "Could Santa be sneaky?
Perhaps he came early and ate the snacks quickly."
"Mac!" cried the friends. "Did Santa come down?"
"The chimney?" Mac shouted. "Nope! He's not around!"

"We'll just make some more," Alpine declared.
"We still have ingredients—enough to be spared."
But as soon as the Boos were done with that batch . . .
They couldn't believe it! The candy was snatched!

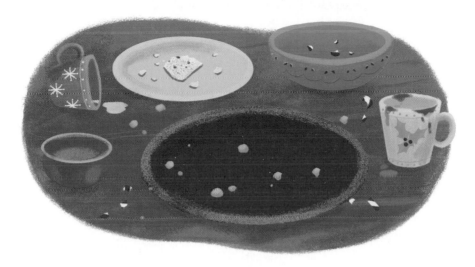

"What's going on?" Freeze asked in dismay.
"Mac! Are you sure Santa's not on his way?"

"Nope!" Mac called,
his voice kind of muffled.
"The chimney is empty.
Not a scrape or a shuffle."

"It's a Christmastime mystery," Comet decided.
"But I think I know how to find out who's behind it."
So the Boos made more gingerbread. It smelled so delicious.
They put the plate on the table, then hid behind the dishes.

They all held their breath and watched,
their eyes open wide.
Would a sneaky Santa Claus be the surprise?

17

Pitter patter came footsteps.
Furry paws grabbed the snack.
The Christmas treat thief was none other than . . .
"Mac!!"

"You caught me," Mac said. "I simply couldn't wait.
I just had to taste them—the treats smelled so great!"
"But what about Santa?" The friends shook their heads.
"Without any cookies, he won't be fed."

"Don't worry!" said Mac. "I didn't forget.
I made a present for Santa—the very best yet."
The Boos followed Mac—he led them on quickly.
Lo and behold, there was a surprise at the chimney.
Mac had indeed taken half of the treats . . .

. . . and used them to build
a Christmas tree made of sweets!

21

"It's perfect!" cried Comet.
"Just lovely," said Freeze.
"You did a great job.
Santa Claus will be pleased."

Little Mac grinned.
"It's all thanks to you.
The treats are delicious . . .
and my tummy's filled, too!"

23

The Christmas clock chimed. It was getting quite late.
It was time for the Boos to head to bed straight.

Everything looked just perfect, a Christmastime sight.
"Merry Christmas to all," said Mac. "And to all a good night."

PO# 610209   © 2016 Ty Inc. Used with permission of Ty Inc.
Snowflakes photo © Created by Freepik